T0121434

WHAT DID WE DO?

THE SURVIVAL OF HUMAN LIFE

YOLANDA C. WILSON-DELLERVA W. COLLINS

authorHOUSE

AuthorHouse™
1663 Liberty Drive
Bloomington, IN 47403
www.authorhouse.com
Phone: 833-262-8899

© 2022 Yolanda C. Wilson-Dellerva W. Collins. All rights reserved.

No part of this book may be reproduced, stored in a retrieval system, or transmitted
by any means without the written permission of the author.

Published by AuthorHouse 10/06/2022

ISBN: 978-1-6655-7203-3 (sc)
ISBN: 978-1-6655-7202-6 (e)

Library of Congress Control Number: 2022917893

Print information available on the last page.

Any people depicted in stock imagery provided by Getty Images are models,
and such images are being used for illustrative purposes only.
Certain stock imagery © Getty Images.

This book is printed on acid-free paper.

Because of the dynamic nature of the Internet, any web addresses or links contained in this book may have changed
since publication and may no longer be valid. The views expressed in this work are solely those of the author and do
not necessarily reflect the views of the publisher, and the publisher hereby disclaims any responsibility for them.

INTRODUCTION

From across the dark waters of Africa to the Carolina cotton fields, true stories of what life was like for Dare County and Hyde County African American Communities during the 1800s persist to the present day. These are stories of heroic men and women who came to America and were sold into enslavement. In this book, you will hear about the struggles of people trying to find humanity, about slaves who made their way to Roanoke Island, NC, and became a part of the freemen's colony.

Native Indians were on Roanoke Island long before the English colony arrived. Algonquian, Cherokee, Mattamuskeet Indians, and other tribes lived in Hyde County and Dare County. Descendants of the Native Indians still live in these areas.

You will meet a ninety-four-year-old woman (at the time of the interview but who lived to be one hundred years old) who tells the story of her childhood, including her life during slavery. She shares her fears during World War II the war that was fought on Roanoke Island. More stories in this book will give you a look into the African American communities. This book has been written with the hope of keeping Dare County's and Hyde County's African

American history alive. I hope this book will be passed down to the next generations to come.

The communities are historical, and the old-timers are passing on. Our ancestors loved each other and their communities. This book tells a small portion of the stories of the lives of those African Americans on Roanoke Island, NC, and in between. We must remember our ancestors' stories by telling them ourselves. The contributions and sacrifices they made helped build such beautiful counties and, by extension, America.

CHAPTER 1

THE BUILDING OF OUR MOTHERLAND

African Royalty

Kings and Queens before Slavery

African history is rich, pure, and holy. It is the start of civilization. African history is the history of humanity. Many Africans were kings and queens, some dating back to the years before Christ. After researching these kings and queens, one famous king, in particular, captured my interest: Mansa Musa. One of the richest men in history, he controlled the valve of gold for the entire Mediterranean. His net worth was estimated to be 400 billion dollars by today's standards. In 1307, he became the ruler of the Mali Empire. Natural resources, like gold and salt, explain why the Mali Empire flourished. It was located in West Africa, and Niani was its capital. Mansa Musa made a pilgrimage to Mecca in 1324, during the seventeenth year of his reign. In the Muslim holy city, he was introduced to rulers in the Middle East and Europe.

The state of Mali stretched across two thousand miles, from the Atlantic

Ocean to Lake Chad. Mansa Musa's leadership ensured decades of peace and prosperity in West Africa. He was given the name Mansa (meaning king) when he was crowned. He was knowledgeable in Arabic and described as a Muslim traditionalist. His pilgrimage to Mecca made him the first Muslim ruler in West Africa to make the nearly four-thousand-mile journey.

The artisans in numerous towns and cities across Mali took years of preparation for the journey. When the pilgrimage began, thousands of escorts went with Musa, and tremendous amounts of gold were brought with them. Some of the gold was distributed to the towns where they traveled. Richly dressed servants and supporters of Musa made generous donations to the poor. In Cairo, Egypt, the emperor gave out so much gold that the entire gold market declined in value, taking a decade to recover. When Mansa Musa returned from Mecca, he brought Arab scholars, government bureaucrats, and architects with him. One architect was named Ishaq El Teudjin. He designed numerous buildings for the emperor. The most famous design was the emperor's chamber in the Malian capital of Niani.

Islamic education in Mali was boosted after Mansa Musa's pilgrimage to Mecca. Mosques, libraries, and universities brought increased commerce, scholars, poets, and artisans to Timbuktu. This made Timbuktu one of the leading cities in the Islamic world. It was the center of Islamic Sub-Saharan Africa. Timbuktu was near the river and Nigeria's most important trading city. It was a trade hub for the West and North African coasts. Salt from the north was a major commodity, as were gold and ivory from the south. By the fifteenth century, the Portuguese were the first to sail down the West African coast. On the African continent, more than eight hundred languages were spoken, and many minerals were mined. Mansa Musa died in 1337, after a twenty-five-year reign. He was succeeded by his son, Maghan.

Africans worked hard and smartly, with much success in building the motherland. As in America, they built domiciles, schools, churches, hospitals, and government buildings. Our people were smart and resourceful and included coal miners and diamond hunters. At the time, molasses was the commodity most in demand. Europeans were no strangers to African trade, and they needed molasses to make rum.

When coal and diamonds were discovered around the country, the landrace was on the way. In the past, the Europeans would trade and leave. Now, with all the coal and diamonds, they came to Africa to trade and stayed around longer. They watched our people in the hope of finding a coal mine or diamonds. They watched Africans work until they learned the African trade. Many people became very rich. Parents saw their children grow up to be kings and queens of various African countries. Our people lived in royalty, with the best of everything. Families had the finest furs, ivory, rubies, and gold.

African history shows that Africans were by no means backward people or inferior to the Europeans, ideas used to justify African slavery. The people who suffered most from the Transatlantic Slave Trade were civilized, organized, and technologically advanced people.

The first of many great African civilizations was Egypt. For thousands of years, Egyptian civilization had incredible achievements in science, mathematics, medicine, technology, and the arts. Kingdoms were dispersed throughout the African landmass. Highly skilled people made objects from bronze, brass, copper, wood, and ivory. Africans were highly skilled in ivory carving, pottery, rope, and gum production, and cowrie shells, kept in a woven purse, were used as a form of currency.

Other important kings in our African history include Akhenaton, Cetewayo, Hannibal, Shaka, Prempeh, Ramesses, and Taharqu. During the slave trade, most of the Africans captured had royal lineage. Just a few include Prince William Ansah Sessarakoo of Ghana, Prince Ayuba Suleiman Diallo of Senegal, Prince Abdulrahman Ibrahim Ibn Sori of Guinea, and King Takyi of Ghana.

West African warrior queens also played an important role in African history. The women of this time were beautiful, strong, brave warriors and queens. Queen Aminatu was a legend among the Hausa people for her military exploits. She ruled for thirty-four years and was an active warrior until her death. She was the first woman to become the Sarauniya queen in a male-controlled society. She represented the spirit and strength of womanhood and was an example of authentic leadership in women.

Another famous queen was Queen Nana Yaa Asantewaa. She was a hero for the people's freedom. She ruled as Queen Mother of Ejisu in the Ashanti Empire, part of modern-day Ghana. She led men of Ashanti, true warriors, to fight the British. She gave her people hope as she promoted peace and reminded them to stand up to injustice. Her people were well cared for, and she advocated for women's rights.

Other famous queens of Africa include Queen Nzinga, Queen Moremi, Queen Sheba, Queen Yaa Asantewa, Queen Nefertiti, and Queen Candace. Princess Aqaltune Ezgodidu Mahamud da Silva Santos of Central Africa was among the royals captured and sold into slavery. Do an online search or go to your public library to learn more about the powerful and fearless kings and queens of our ancestry.

This chapter is an introduction to key African achievers, and heroes of their time, who made significant contributions despite great obstacles. Their roles in world history cannot be understated. The ancient name for "Africa" was Alkebulan, meaning "Mother of Mankind" or "Garden of Eden."

Our children need to know their African heritage. It will help them identify with who they are, where they came from, and where they can go. We cannot forget the pain and anguish our forefathers endured to make this continent what it is today, where human beings were classified as less than human, and less than citizens, for hundreds of years.

As history charts its course, people alter that course, and our African

American children are robbed of that which connects them to their ancestry and heritage-rich culture. It is a history of courage, strength, patience, and fortitude—a history of proud African people.

There are four things that our ancestors have held onto even to this day—faith in God, prayer, love of family, and education.

CHAPTER 2

FROM CELEBRATION TO AGGRAVATION

Families Fight to Find Freedom

It was a scorching day in our African Native land. A young couple had just got married in a village. It was the ceremony of life, of two coming together as one.

George and Jane loved each other very much. After jumping over the broom, the celebration marked the start of a beautiful day. The sound of music sounded throughout the kingdom as if dancing in the air as the people celebrated. They must have danced for hours.

Jane's parents were both dead, her father by a wild animal while out hunting, and her mother while giving birth to her. She was raised by her aunt, who had passed away five months before the wedding. George's parents, Mary and Benjamin, were both at the celebration. In the kingdom, his parents were known as the top elders of the village. The wedding suggested they were royalty, and the celebration included the best of everything they had.

After a wonderful day, everyone returned to his or her village and country homes to rest. Word spread quickly in the kingdom about the white men and other African tribes who had come at night as they slept. They were all so afraid of the tricks the white man brought with him. They knew it was not in their best interest. There were rumors of beatings, killings, and kidnappings of our youth. All they could do was pray to their God, keeping their hope and faith that Almighty God would protect them from what had come to do them harm.

Things soon got so bad that George and Jane had to leave and hide. They had to leave behind George's parents and the other elders of the kingdom and go to the hills to hide. The elders were left behind because they were not able to climb. This broke George's heart so badly that he almost stayed—until his father told him he had to protect Jane. It was his duty. When night came, George and Jane said their goodbyes and headed toward the hills.

At night, they were cold and afraid, trembling at the sounds emerging from the dark of night. As daylight approached, we tried our best to stay out of sight as we tried to find food and water. We saw our family members and friends walk into traps blue-eyed men had set to conquer our people, traps designed to catch animals. We had no idea what they wanted or where they were taking our young men, women, and children.

Days and nights passed. My new bride and I remained hidden in the hills. We can hear the sound of people screaming, crying, and fighting for their lives. As we looked into each other's eyes, we could feel the fear of what might happen to us. We decided to make a vow to each other: no matter what happened, we would fight to stay together, and our love for one another would live forever. As George kissed Jane, tears rolled down her beautiful face. For a moment, time seemed to stop, and no one else was around. We found ourselves making out under an old oak tree.

Daylight approached once again, marking another day we had managed to escape the hands of the blue-eyed white man. The enemies were getting closer, and we had nowhere left to hide. We could hide up in the trees, but somehow, they could still find us. The men who were after us were all over the hills. By now, hundreds—perhaps thousands—of our people had been caught. George discovered the reason they were after us: the slave trade. Our people were being kidnapped and sold by men who spoke a different language than the people from our homeland.

Days and nights passed as George and Jane remained in the hills, not knowing when they would be caught. One day, while going to look for water, we got lost. We couldn't find our way back to the place we had hidden for the previous days. We had just stopped to rest when five or more men descended upon us. Here we were, face to face with the blue-eyed white man. As the men pointed guns at us, two other men chained us together, walking us out of the hill to the shoreline.

Out in the hot sun by the sea, our people are chained by the hundreds. You can hear the sound of people crying. The white men are waiting for a ship to pull up. When the boat arrives and anchors down, our people are forced onto the boat. We cannot understand what they are saying. We will never forget the awful smell throughout the boat—the smell of evil, the smell of death.

Our journey seems to take a month. We are chained two by two by our hands and feet, through ringbolts fastened to the deck. We were confined in this manner for the duration of the journey. We had maybe one pint of water a day. Twice a day, we were fed yams and horse beans. Some of the captives refused to eat or drink, wishing to die rather than live in such horrific conditions. Slave traders would force open their mouths with a device called a speculum to feed them. After meals, we were made to jump in the chains. If someone did not jump, the slave trader would whip the person. The girls and women were forced to dance without their clothes for the captain. If refused, they were whipped.

Women, men, and children died every day, some killed at the hand of the slave traders, others of suffocation. We spend most hours each day below deck without a breath of fresh air. The smell on the ship is the stench of death. As the people died, the slave traders would keep the dead hanging from their chains, the bodies hanging there until they had rotted. Bodies were kept below deck with the living. We had about two hundred captives on the ship. At least one hundred perished before the end of the journey. When the captain got sick of smelling rotting flesh, he instructed the crew to throw the dead bodies overboard into the sea.

Months passed, it seemed. Finally, we reached our destination. As we pulled into port, the crew became very excited. They had completed the long journey, traversing dark waters with a shipful of African slaves to sell.

Shackled together two by two, we were led off the ship. We were now in a new world, a place much different from what we were used to. The land was so unknown to us. Being on the ship so long, we had picked up some of the slave traders' language. We heard them say we were in a place called "Wilmington, NC," located on the "Cape Fear River."

This is where George and Jane were sold. After being taken off the ship, we were told to line up. Some were naked as they alit the ship; others wore scant clothing, most of it torn. They took a bucket of water and threw it at us, trying to wash away the terrible stench that stuck to us all. The men were given a shirt and pants, the women a dress. After everyone was "cleaned up," we were told to stay in line until we were called. When they called you, you would walk across a plank for men to look you over. The men came from everywhere to buy slaves. They looked over us as if we were cattle, deciding whether to buy.

Jane and I prayed we would remain together. Some families were split up, never to see each other again. It was a pitiful sight. God answered our prayers that day, as we were sold together as husband and wife. We were looked over like cattle and told we would be suitable for breeding.

We were still in the hands of strangers. We were told to get on the back of a horse and cart. It took a day or more before we reached the stranger's house.

Here, we were met by two older slaves. The stranger told the slaves to take us to where we would be sleeping. Before he left, he told the slaves to ensure we all had a hot meal and a hot bath.

"They stink," he said to the slaves.

The elder couple replied, "Yes, master."

The stranger walked up to the big house. We went to a small shack in the back of the big house. The couple gave us clean clothes and showed us where to take a bath. As we bathed, a hot meal was prepared for us. While eating our meal, the couple told us about how they were kidnapped from Africa and the kingdom whence they came, how they were stolen and sold into slavery. The couple had been on this farm for more than ten years. They said we must stop calling the man who brought us here a stranger. We all call him "master." He is the master who gave you a place to stay, food to eat, and clothes on your back. As long as you did what the master told you to do, everything would be all right. If you didn't do as he said, you could be beaten or even killed. The old man said never to run away. This would always turn out bad for you. As long as you did what was asked of you, he would protect you.

As the man grew quiet, you could see the pain on his face.

The old man pulled up his shirt to show us his back. His scarred back told a story of hatred and control. He had been whipped as a young man for running away. He said he was lucky he wasn't killed. The older couple told us God would look after us just as he did in Africa, as long as we kept our faith and hope for a better day and prayed everything would be all right and improve for all our people.

He showed us where to sleep for the night, telling us to get some rest. The day would come fast, and the master wanted us in the fields before the sun rose. We rested in a small room, with a bed to lie down on. Before going to sleep, we dropped to our knees and thanked God he had kept us together and we were both still alive. We ask God to be with us and our people and keep us safe from all evil.

It was now dawn, and the sun was creeping up into the sky. It was my first day on land. The couple we met told us what our jobs on the big farm would be. George was sent to the fields to plow and plant crops. Jane was told to go up to the big house to help with the cooking, cleaning, and caring for the master's wife and children.

George and Jane worked from sunup to sundown. They hardly saw each other until late at night. On the first day in the field, George saw people from his native kingdom in Africa. The men and women told him stories from back home in Africa. He was told the entire kingdom he had come from was destroyed when it was ambushed by the blue-eyed white man. All the people, young and old, were killed. George's heart was broken. Tears rolled down his face, and he asked about his parents, sister, and brother whom he had left behind. He heard his parents had died. During the ambush, the elders were killed first, and the kingdom was set on fire. It was unknown what had happened to his two sisters and brother. George started to cry harder, his heart seeming to break into a million pieces, about to fall out of his chest.

As the other slaves tried to comfort George, they told him the master could never hear them tell stories of their native land and to take care no one heard him telling Jane. One of the slaves gave him a drink of water and said, "Let's get back to work before the master notices us." George and other slaves said a pray under an old oak tree and returned to work in the fields.

George was a tall, strong, intelligent, handsome man with dark skin. That day, he decided that whatever the master asked of him, he would do. He knew if people could kill other people out of hate, as his parents were in their eighties, he too could be killed. He didn't want anything to happen to take him away from his love, Jane. She was all the family he had left. On his first day in the field, George worked hard. The master watched George all day as he worked and was very pleased with what he saw.

That night, as George and Jane got ready for bed, George told Jane about the people he had seen in the field. He told Jane what had happened in Africa after they left. Jane held tightly to George as he told her about the ambush in Africa. When telling Jane about the killings and our kingdom burning, she cried, begging God for mercy for the people of Africa, saying to God, "Our people have been taken into darkness. We need to see the light."

George held Jane tighter to him as he wiped the tears away from her face. As he kissed her on the forehead, he said, "I will lay down my life for you.

I'm your husband. I will do everything in my power, with God's guidance, to find a better way for us. I promise you, I will. It has to be a better way for us, Jane. I promise you I will find a way for us."

Years had now passed; it had been so long that I had lost count of how long we had been here. The husband and wife we met when we arrived at the farm had passed away. The man we called master had been good to us. We had always done what the master asked of us. He gave us a place of our own to live shortly after we came to the farm. We had food to eat every day. The master provided us with new shoes twice a year, clothes, and a coat for the cold once a year. When the master was good, he was very good. We knew when the master was angry about something, and we knew to stay out of his way. We saw the evil side come out of him many times. If slaves didn't do as he had instructed, they would pay the price.

One day, a young slave tried to escape. Master sent the dogs, trained to hunt humans, out to pick up the trail. Most of the time, other slaves would have to help catch the runaway slave. That same day, the young boy was caught. He was about fifteen years old. The boy had run before. The boy was brought back to the farm. The master ordered two slave men to hang the young runaway from a tree. The master made all the men, women, and child slaves come out to look when the boy was whipped. It was the most horrible thing we had ever seen. He was whipped so badly, that the boy's flesh fell off his body. I believe the boy was already dead when the master told the men to set his body on fire. It was the most gruesome thing we had ever seen. Sometimes, it took days to find a runaway slave, and sometimes, slaves would get away, never to be seen again, fleeing anywhere they might find freedom.

George and Jane seemed to have protection around them from God. They were never beaten, and the two prayed and thanked God every day, many times a day and night. Jane recalled a time when one of the slaves stole a ham out of the master's smokehouse. The master found out she had done it and cut off three of her fingers. She was told he would kill her if she ever stole from him again. Although the master was good to us, life was hard.

Jane and George wanted a child but were afraid of what could happen to a child born into slavery. Jane prayed day and night, asking God not to let her get pregnant. Jane knew her child would be the property of the master. Slave children were used for hard labor to enrich the future of the master's family.

Jane had seen other pregnant slave women still having to work hard, long hours at the big house. They worked hard up to the moment their baby was born. A few days after giving birth, the women had to return to work. The baby came with the mother so she could breastfeed. Their maternal duties could not interfere with the domestic tasks of cooking, cleaning, washing, ironing, caring for the master's three children, and helping the master's wife with anything she needed. Most of the time, the master was satisfied. The women knew they had to keep up with their duties. When a child turned one, he or she could no longer come to the big house with their mother. The oldest slaves, too old to work the farm, looked after the slave children who were too young to work the farm. Jane knew this was no life for any child. Deep in her heart, she knew life would somehow get better.

Rumors spread of an impending war. Many of the slaves were tired of their living conditions and treatment. Slaves were fed up with being beaten with whips, having limbs cut off, seeing families torn apart, and particularly seeing their women raped as they were forced to watch, unable to do a thing about it. They were treated less humanely than animals.

We emerged from our shacks in the morning to find our people hanging from trees. Usually, we didn't know who they were or where they came from. The master would tell us to cut the person down and bury them in a field at the back of the farm. The master had a graveyard on his property for the slaves, as did many other slave owners.

Tension is growing on the farm. The war is about to break out, and the master must leave to fight in the war. We were afraid of what might happen. Perhaps we would all be killed. White people started to fear the slaves, thinking we were plotting to kill them and take over. White people knew a man would rather die a free man than be enslaved.

Some slaves ran to find freedom, while others remained on the farm. George and Jane decided to stay, feeling this was safer for now. The master had left to fight in the war with the Confederate Army. The master was fighting a war to keep life as we knew it. The master was afraid he would lose more than one hundred slaves. After the master left, things got harder for the slaves who remained on the farm. Food was reduced to almost nothing, mere scraps from the big house. The master's wife didn't give out any food to the slaves. Only white folk kept the food. We did the best we could with what little we had. We were no longer allowed to farm and grow the food we ate. Many of the slaves had left the farm, seeking a safe place to live as free people. As time passed, food stores continued to dwindle. George feared his family might starve to death. He had heard about slaves who had helped other slaves run away to freedom.

Late that night, George met with a group deep in the woods. He was told that the trip would be safe and that every runaway had found the way to freedom. George knew there was a chance they could be killed. It was a chance George was willing to take for the freedom of his family. George continued to meet with the secret group, and Jane knew nothing about the escape until the time to run had come.

At the final meeting, George met the group's leader, who helped the families to freedom. When the leader emerged from around the trees, to George's surprise, it was a five-foot, three-inch woman. Everyone was calling her the "Freedom Rider." She told the men were to bring their families, what paths to take, what to listen for, and what time to start. She also told them who to look for, what to stay clear of, and where we would find food, money, and safe places to stay on our way. She said the places where we were going, the people know her as the "Freedom Rider." She warned us there would be no going back once we had reached the first destination; if necessary, she would kill us herself for the safety of the other slaves. Later, they would all learn her real name: Harriet Tubman.

The time had come for George to tell Jane about the escape. He sat her down in the dark one-room shack George had built out of old wood and tin the master did not need. As he told her the plan, she was understandably wary, but she put her faith in God and George's decision. She began gathering what little belongings they had.

As the darkness of night came, George and Jane listened for the sound of an owl—Harriet used this as a signal it was time to go. When the sound was heard, George and Jane ran as fast as they could with the little they had. When everyone got there, it was no time to waste. They moved quickly through the woods behind the master's farmhouse. As we ran, we got deeper and deeper into the woods. We must have run and walked for hours. When Harriet got us to a safe place, she split the runaways up. Some white families were helping Harriet get us to freedom. George and Jane were sent to an old farm, where there was so much land you could hardly see the barn. We stayed in the barn, never coming back out for anything. We stayed there until getting word it was time to move on. Enough water and food were given to us to last three days. A tall, blue-eyed white man and his wife came and got us out of the barn and took us up to their house, where a horse with a covered-top wagon was waiting. We got on the back and covered ourselves out of sight.

We were now far away from our master's farm. We are on our way to freedom. The people never told us their names; it was a part of their secret mission. We were taken to a house, where we hid for four days in a cellar. We were given hot meals and got to take a nice hot bath. The kind people gave us clean clothes to put on. White families were helping to make an underground road to bring slaves to freedom. The lady told us about a place called Roanoke Island. She said the Union Army had set up a camp there and was taking in free blacks and runaway slaves to help build and cook for the Union Army. She said if we could cross the creek onto Roanoke, we would become free. We were told the Union would keep us safe, give us food to eat, and provide a place to stay. We had to walk through the woods going north. We were given food and some money, after which they prayed for our safety.

George felt in his heart that he was closer to bringing his family to freedom. He knew how many days it would take before they came to a fork in the road. He thought about the lady telling him to stay north, following the North Star. She had told him it would be late at night when we crossed the creek onto Roanoke Island. After crossing the creek, we had to walk two miles north. As we walked, it was as if the moon's light led us straight to the fort. When we reached the Union Army camp, we were welcomed into the fort. They gave us a hot meal to eat and dry clothes to wear. Before closing their eyes to sleep, George and Jane fell to their knees to pray and give thanks to the Lord for their freedom.

The next day, George worked alongside the Union soldiers in the building known as Fort Raleigh. Jane helped cook, wash, and sew the torn uniforms of the soldiers. The Union Army was led by General Ambrose E. Burnside and had fifteen thousand US Army troops. General Ambrose had plans to capture the island. The Federals had a base to attack the Confederates in North Carolina from the sea. The Confederates had about three thousand soldiers under Colonel Henry M. Shaw and flag officer William F. Lynch. Supporting them were a three-gun battery and seven gunboats. Three forts stood on the northwest part of the twelve-mail-long island. Lynch was definitely by Burnside, having to surrender near the northern tip of Roanoke Island.

The war was one of the bloodiest battles anyone had ever seen. Ships had been blown up in the water, and dead bodies had started floating to the shoreline, numbering in the hundreds. The free slaves dug graves to entomb the unknown bodies. The sound stayed bloody for a long time. Although life as a free man was somewhat better than what we had experienced in the past, our future was still uncertain. The Union Army gave us land to build, and we grew some of our food to eat. We began to build homes to live in, churches to pray, and schools to give our children a place to read and write. As free men, we knew the fight was not over. The loud sound of the cannonballs going off, the smell of the muster guns, and all the dead bodies stayed with us long after the war was over.

The war was turning from a war between the North and South to a fight for freedom for all enslaved people. The time had come for us to prove ourselves. The Union had lost a lot of men and needed more men to fight in the war. White people called us colored people, so the Union started to enlist free colored men into the Union Army. The men enlisted, thinking it would give them the opportunities to make a better life for their families. Many had come from West Africa and were used to fighting. The men had been doing drills together to stay fit, and in practice, just in case, they had to fight to keep their freedom. The free slaves used corn stalks, pretending they were weapons. We did these drills every day, pretending we were in a real battle.

The free men had left behind their wives and children. Fighting with the Union Army, white men refused to fight alongside what they called colored men. When they came to America, African men and women worked tough jobs without pay. They put sweat and tears into the labor it took to build our beautiful nation.

George fought in the war with the Union Army until it was over. He returned to the island and made it home for his family, who live there to this day. After coming home, George opened up his own cobbler shop. This is how he made his living. Whites and African Americans came to his shop to have their shoes made or repaired. George had learned the trade in Africa from his father.

Slavery and the war were over, and our lives were somewhat better. We had our freedom, but we still had to be careful of ourselves. Jane found domestic work and helped George in his shop when she could. One day, Jane told George she was praying to have a child. George was happy to hear she was asking God to give them a child. During slavery, they had prayed *not* to have one. Time passed, and soon, Jane was pregnant. George started gathering wood so he could make Jana a cradle for the baby.

Jane gave birth to a girl named Chloe J. Wise. Her birthplace is unknown, as is much else about Chloe. We do know that on December 28, 1872, she gave birth to a healthy baby boy named John Frank Wise. His father was James D. Midgett. After the baby was born, life wasn't easy for them. George, his grandfather, did all he could to keep a roof over their heads and food on the table.

As John Frank got older, George taught his grandson all about shoemaking and repair, just as his father had passed it down to him. George hoped that one day, he and John Frank could run his shoe shop together. John was always under his grandfather, and he learned how to work with an anvil/ shoe last, it is used to determine the shape of the shoe. This shoe last is still part of the family, along with his wooden shoe block.

John could cut patterns out of cardboard used to cut the leather or fabric to assemble the shoes. His awl is another tool my family still holds dear to our hearts; it was used to mark leather and punch holes. As John got older, he worked in the shop with his grandfather. Shoemaking became a joy for John, giving him a sense of pride in his work. His customers were always pleased with him and his work. John was a quiet, humble man. When John's grandparents passed away, John went to live with his father, James Midgett. The name Wise came from John's mother and grandparents. John loved his family and missed them very much.

As time went on, John met the love of his life, a beautiful young Indian girl who had fallen in love with him, as he had with her. Before going to war, John found the courage one day to ask her father if he could marry his daughter. Her father knew John to be a prominent man on the island. Joseph and Annie gave their blessings to John and their daughter, Edna.

John's father fell sick with smallpox. John Frank would not let anyone go near his father, not even his wife, who made soup for James. Smallpox was very contagious, but John Frank took care of his father until his death. John Frank and his wife ran the shoe shop, and John taught his wife about the trade. You will hear more about John Frank and his wife in upcoming chapters. George had given his grandson the strength and the courage to face whatever he might need to endure. George and Jane made it to Roanoke Island. To make it to the island, you needed to be a survivor. George, Jane, Chloe, and John

Frank Wise became a part of the story of the Freedmen's Colony, a safe place for runaway slaves and free blacks. Records were not kept of the tribes and homelands of African slaves, so it is impossible to know the ethnic makeup of North Carolina's slave population.

CHAPTER 3

NATIVE INDIAN

A Family **Story**

North Carolina was settled in the 1500s. The Cherokee, Tuscarora, Catawba, Hatteras, Cortana, and other Natives had been here long before Christopher Columbus and Sir Walter Raleigh claimed to have discovered America. In North Carolina, there were three large tribes. The Cherokee is one of the largest groups of Indians. The Tuscarora and the Catawba are the smallest groups.

Cherokee Indians once occupied an area of about 140,000 square miles, which became part of North Carolina. The Cherokee thrived in North Carolina into the late eighteenth century. As white settlers moved into and near Cherokee lands, conflicts between the two arose. The contact whites brought was war, disease, and enslavement to the Cherokee people.

Coastal tribes tried to avoid fate by adapting to white culture. The US Federal government responded to the demands of land-hungry whites, and

North Carolina forcibly removed the Cherokees from their land. Cherokees lost their lives on the Trail of Tears. Many of the Indians on Roanoke Island refused to leave their homes and land. So many lives were lost that the government decided to let the Indians who had remained keep their land.

After the Trail of Tears, the government had Indians register for social security cards and identify themselves as American citizens. Our grandmother's parents were full-blooded Cherokee Indians. Her people had no written language. Our grandmother had to show proof of her birth. There was no proof anywhere, not even in an old family Bible. It took months to get her a card. Finally, the SS office sent her two years of birth to choose from; she chose the one that made her the youngest.

When paperwork returned to the Indians, their race was listed as Negro. The natives lost their culture and the way of life they were used to before their land was stolen. Their God-given birthright would never be returned. Indians were told never to speak their native language or they would be killed; they had to learn to speak English. Our grandma would sometimes speak her native language, and her daughter, Dellerva Wise Collins, would tell her to stop before the wrong person heard, as she might have been killed.

Our grandmother could not read or write. When signing names, she and her husband signed their name with an X. As young girls, my cousin Ruth Edna and I taught our grandmother how to write the alphabet and numbers as well as how to write her name. She worked at the Manteo post office, located in downtown Manteo for over fourteen years.

It was told that Grandma's family was proud of her for marrying John Frank. He and his grandfather were shoemakers. They had the only place on the island where one could buy or repair shoes. Grandmothers got married at the age of fourteen in the Union. They had six children: Hettie Wise (1920–1948), John Grant Wise (1925–1947), William Stanley Wise (1930–1946), Sabra Wise Tillett (1927–1995), Elwood Wise (1932–1996), Dellerva Wise Collins (1934–2005), their mother, Edna May Bowser Wise (1905–1996), and father, John Frank Wise (1872–1934).

To this day, the Bowser families in Dare County are descendants of these brave men and women who refused to leave their homes and land. Some of the families still own the same land; others were stolen or taken away from the families by the county for property taxes.

My grandmother Edna May Bowser Wise was the daughter of Joseph Bowser and Annie Allen Bowser and the wife of John Frank Wise, about whom you will read in chapter 6. Her father was one of the brave Indian men who resisted the removal and stayed on the land. An 1850 slave census showed that 80 percent were Indians. There were 88 families, totaling 610 people: 168 slaves and 26 free blacks. Some of the slave owners on Roanoke Island were Asby, Baum, Cudworth, Daniels, Dough, Etheridge, Midgett, Owens, Pugh, Tillett, Wise, and Ward.

Edna's grandfather worked on the farm of Daniel and Nancy Cudworth. The enslaved men on the island farmed, cut timber, tended livestock, mended nets, hunted, and served as watermen. The census around 1850 to 1860 shows that the Bowsers were not free black people but Native Indians who had been on the land long before the 1800s.

As children, our grandmother Edna loved to sit around with the children and tell stories about her Indian childhood. Indians had no hand in written language to keep the family history. Storytelling is a tradition to keep Indians' past alive so it might be passed down from generation to generation. Our grandmother told us how she had lived on the island all her life. She called her father "Papa." You could hear the pride and love she had for him and her momma as she talked about them. When she speaks about where she grew up, she is referring to today's Bowsertown road in Manteo, NC.

The people who lived in Bowsertown were mostly Indians. They were all related; most were Bowsers or Tillett's. My great-grandparents' home was near the sound. The home setting is now in Dare County Mosquito control, on Bowsertown road, in Manteo, NC. When I was a little girl, the house was still standing. No one lived there for a long time. My grandmother would occasionally visit the old home. One day, she came out with a few things she had found that she wished to keep. She had found an 1800 dime, a 1900 penny, and a confederate button. Her family still has these items.

"That sound over there keeps us with food to eat," she said.

The children went into the woods to find wild berries and acorns. Her papa had his garden, which had squash, corn, beans, peas, and melons. He also fished and hunted. She recalled eating a lot of rabbits, and she would laugh. An apple and a pear tree were on the land. Sassafras and mint grew wild. Annie, my grandmother, Edna's mother, would make sassafras mint tea for her family.

My grandmother never forgot the customs of the Indian people. She gave her grandchildren the pleasure of tasting and enjoying her delicious iced sassafras mint tea. Our grandmother tried to hold on to as much of her heritage as possible. She was an excellent homemaker. She made beautiful quilts out of our old clothes. She was also an extraordinary cook. This skill was passed down to her from her mother and grandmother, whom she said taught her.

Indians lived on the Outer Banks of North Carolina as far back as 1500, long before North Carolina was set. The Cherokee, Tuscarora, Catawba, Hatteras, Cortana, and other Native Americans had been here long before. Indian names have been changed many times in history.

Intelligent and resourceful, the Bowser women were jacks-of-all-trades. Edna had a granddaughter, born on February 11, 1944. Born prematurely, she weighed only 4 pounds. Dr. Johnson was the only doctor at this time. One day, the doctor called the family into his office to tell them there was nothing more he could do. The baby would die, he said. At the time, Joseph's mother, Jane, was still alive. The women asked if they could bring the baby home with them. The doctor said it would be fine, so the woman brought the baby home wrapped in a blanket. They put her in a wooden crate and placed the baby behind a wooden stove. The baby was named Josephine Wise Parks. She stayed behind the stove, not coming out until after spring. She was fed, bathed, and changed all behind the stove. She still lives to this day. We like to say our grandmothers invented the first incubator.

Grandma is what we called her, and she had many trades she had learned from her parents. She grew her fruit and vegetables and canned food throughout the summer season. In the winter, her family would enjoy the canned apples that she used to make apple turnovers (served with vanilla ice cream) or mouth-melting homemade peach cobbler. These were some of her best Sunday desserts. At breakfast, we had her hot buttermilk or sweet potato biscuits, made from scratch, served with her preserved figs.

Our grandma raised chickens, and we ate the eggs and the chicken when they got big enough. Growing up, my brother, Darrell, was the only male in the home. grandfather John Frank was deceased, as were Darrell and my father, Frank Collins, who served and lost his life in the United States Coast Guard doing hurricane Donna in 1960. Sometimes, the girls just couldn't handle all the chores and a man was needed. Darrell would step in to help he had fun going outside with Grandma to catch a chicken and wring its neck. Then, Grandma would clean and pull the feathers off the chicken. That night, we would have delicious chicken potpie pastry, made from scratch. Oh, so good. Her meals were the best and made with love. It made her heart sing and laugh. The Holy Spirit would overcome her with joy at the knowledge that her family had been fed. It brought her so much joy that she would laugh in the spirit.

We were poor, but we ate like royals—soft shell crabs, shrimp, and ducks at Christmastime. Our uncle, Sam Moor Sr., was married to Edna's sister Annie. He raised cattle, and he would take them off to be slaughtered. When he returned home with the meat, it would fill the kitchen. The meat was shared with the world family. Aunt Annie's was another place where you would have a delicious meal. The sisters would get together to cook and bake. They made beautiful fruitcakes and pound cakes from scratch, which would melt in your mouth.

Edna's parents, Joseph and Annie, had six children—Edna May Bowser Wise, Irene Bowser Scarborough, Elizabeth Bowser Scarborough, Dorothy Bowser Purvis, Hazel Pearl Bowser Scarborough, Annie Bowser Moore, and John Boyd Bowser. The children of the sisters live on the island to this day. Currently, Louis Spencer is the oldest living member of the Bowser family. She is the daughter of James and Dorothy Bowser Purvis.

CHAPTER 4

THE FIRST SLAVES BROUGHT TO DARE COUNTY

A **Voyage** to Ocracoke and Hatteras, North Carolina

The first Africans arrived on Hatteras Island on the Outer Banks of North Carolina during the early 1700s. The slaves were brought from Virginia and Maryland. In 1790, the census showed that 135 whites, 2 free persons of color, and 31 slaves lived in Ocracoke, NC. By the Civil War, the population of slaves in Ocracoke, NC, numbered more than one hundred. After the war, the slaves left the island. During the post–Civil War period, the first African American family moved to Ocracoke, making it home for one hundred years.

In 1867, Harkus and Winnie Bragg Blount moved to Ocracoke with a white family, the Williams. Winnie was born into slavery. She and Harkus are believed to come from the Blount plantation, near Washington, NC. Harkus was a carpenter and boat builder. Winnie did domestic work. The couple had thirteen children, but only two daughters made it to adulthood, Jane and

Annie Laura Blount. The couple managed to purchase land along Lighthouse Road in Ocracoke, NC. The dates of Harkus's birth and death are unknown. Winnie was born in 1825; she died in 1925.

Researching and writing this story was fascinating. One African man chose to bring his family to an island where no other African lived. One could believe that Harkus and Winnie were chosen by God to demonstrate to the world, not just America, that people of different races can live together in peace and harmony. With all the hard work, sweat, and tears, Harkus and Winnie had been through, Harkus still made time for romance, siring thirteen children. Harkus couldn't bring his family to the beach to swim during the daylight hours when white people were enjoying the warm sunlight. Harkus would plan a romantic night on the beach for his wife. Hidden in the dunes was a blanket laid down on the sand with fruit and tea for Winnie. Still able to see the children, he swept Winnie off her feet into the dunes to sit and talk under the stars.

It was truly a story of love, faith, and courage, living on an island populated entirely by white folks at a time when a man of color could be lynched. The Ku Klux Klan was thriving, and what we now recognize as hate crimes went unpunished. Harkus knew Ocracoke was a piece of paradise here on earth, with the white-sand beaches, the sound of the sea, and the beauty of the sound. He knew he could find work there so he could feed his family. What better place to be after coming out of slavery?

History shows that most African American families carry the slaveholder's last name. From 1752 to 1833, John Blount and his brother founded a trading and shipping company in Washington, NC. Together, John Blount and his brother owned more than three hundred slaves. The brothers built a commercial enterprise for the Blounts—gristmills, lumber mills, and cotton and tobacco plantations. The family had attorneys, real estate speculation, and much more from Boston to Tennessee and from Alabama to the West Indies. The slaves, held against their will, provided free labor. Washington, NC, was one of the busiest ports in the state. With deep water, it was 80 miles east on a straight line to Ocracoke, NC. Land in Ocracoke was purchased by John Blount, who renamed it Shell Castle Island. Construction materials came to the island. In a year, Shell Castle Island was operational. I encourage you to research and learn more about one of the wealthiest white men in the state of North Carolina.

In the late 1800s, a young businessman named Henry Doxsee arrived from Long Island, New York. The operation was a factory specializing in fish and seafood, especially clams. His father, James Doxsee, established a factory where he could produce clam chowder, whole clams, and clam juice. Clams in New York had diminished, so Henry moved the main operation to Ocracoke, NC. Close to the Pamlico Sound, a plant was built. It became known as Doxsee's. Young unmarried women and widows were hired to pick clams. The clams were steamed, cooled, and then poured onto wooden tables. After the death of Harkus, Winnie and her daughter Jane worked at Doxsee's. You can learn more about James Harvey Doxsee online or at your public library.

On a hot summer day, a handsome young man walked into Doxsee looking for work. A nice young lady caught his eye before he left and politely said hello. The young lady was Jane. He had caught her eye as well. That day, Jane looked around to see if the man was still at the factory. The next morning, the man was back. Jane felt nervous because the man was walking straight toward her. He said, "Good morning, ma'am. My name is Leonard Bryant. I'm here to see Ms. Doxsee. May I ask what your name is?"

She answered, "I'm Jane Blount. Mr. Doxsee is back there in the back room."

Jane walked away to join her mother at work as she glanced back at Leonard.

Leonard Bryant was a Native Indian from Blounts Creek, a town in Beaufort County, NC. He was born in the area in 1879. At that time, the land was occupied by two Indian tribes, or maybe even nations. When white colonists came along, Indians had to adopt a new way of life. Leonard had moved to Engelhard, NC, before taking the job in Ocracoke. He was a waterman. He built homes and had fruit and vegetables he grew to sell. Leonard was a well-dressed, polite, religious man with a good sense of humor, always finding the good in things.

Leonard would catch the ferry from Engelhard to Ocracoke to work at the Doxsee's. He worked there until the factory closed down. Throughout the first year, Jane came to know Leonard well. Her mother, Winnie, was pleased with the blossoming relationship between her daughter and Leonard. Winnie knew he was a good man and could see how much he loved Jane. Winnie knew it wasn't long before he would ask her for Jane's hand in marriage. When the time did come, Winnie couldn't be happier; she told all the people on the small island that her daughter and Leonard were getting married. The townspeople thought highly of Winnie and did all they could to make the wedding a special day. On the wedding day, ladies from the village presented a beautiful wedding cake, and Winnie made a seafood dinner with vegetables from Leonard's garden, homemade cornbread, and iced tea. This was the start of an incredible romance. Out of their union, it is said that they raised thirteen children on Ocracoke Island, NC.

The children are the grandchildren of Harkus and Winnie Blount, the start of the hundred-plus years of the Blount-Bryant legacy. At the beginning of Leonard and Jane's marriage, they would catch the ferry to Engelhard, a town across the water from Ocracoke but still in the same county. Today, the Blount and Bryant families still live in Hyde County. Leonard had a brother he would visit while in Engelhard; his brother's name was Len, and his wife was Betsy Bryant. Leonard would bring vegetables and fruit he had grown. Betsy always had canned preserves and pickles. One of Jane's favorites was Betsy's watermelon rind preserves, which one could enjoy as a sweet treat by itself, on hot biscuits, or with pan-fried cornbread. People in those days had very little, and families shared what they had with each other.

Leonard and Jane started their family in the early 1900s. Leonard loved Jane with all his heart. When Jane would walk away, he would softly pat her on her butt, one of his ways of showing his affection. They owned their land and home in Ocracoke. As Jane's mother, Winnie, became older and couldn't live alone, she lived with her daughter, Leonard, and her grandchildren. Jane cared for her mother until she passed away in 1925, at the age of ninety-four. Jane missed her mother and father deeply. Jane always held on to their memory by teaching her children about them. Leonard passed in 1960, and Jane passed in 1964—both lived to be in their eighties.

Their last living child in Ocracoke was Muzzle Bryant, born in 1904 and passing in 2008, at 104. At this time, no Bryant or Blount lived on the island, but the two families now live in Engelhard, NC. Len Bryant, Leonard's brother, has a granddaughter named Iris Bryant Murray; her mother was Ivy Dean Bryant, who passed away in 2010. Iris and her husband live in the home her grandparents built. Her mother and uncles were proud of their rich heritage.

I'm glad to have met Ms. Ivy Dean. She was a sweet, kind lady with a lot of great wisdom. I dedicate this part of the chapter to Ms. Ivy Dean Bryant, her daughter, Iris Bryant Murray, and her husband, Donnie, for their support in sharing their family history. The white families of Ocracoke, NC, back then and now are true warriors as well, demonstrating that humanity is the first law of nature, something we all need to have as a part of our character to pass down to future generations.

This family story came from a journalism class I took in ninth grade, between 1975 and 1976. Our end-of-the-year assignment was to discover who was the oldest person living in our communities at the time. We had to interview and write a report about that person. In my community, it was Mrs. Cora Tillett Scarborough, born in 1882, called Granny by her family.

Granny was age ninety-four at the time of the interview. I started by asking her to go back as far as she could remember. She went back to when she was only seven years old. She remembered being put on a ship with her parents and the following voyage, which seemed to take months.

She said, "I'm not sure I was so young, but I believe we came from Canada. We were used to hearing Spanish- and French-speaking people. The men who forced them on a ship speak a different language. She believed they were Portuguese."

I asked her if her family had been chained together. Shaking her head in sorrow, she said, "Yes, they ever had one small enough to fit me." Her family was brought to Cape Hatteras, NC. The family was taken to Camden, NC. Cotton farms and cotton mills operated in North Carolina from 1838 until the mills closed. In the 1960s cotton farms were still plentiful throughout

Currituck and Camden NorthCarolina.The family was there for some time until her father found a way to move his family to Manteo, NC.

"Granny's mind was still sharp." She talked about the war on the island back in 1942. This was World War II, the battle for control of the sea. North Carolina and the Outer Banks were on the frontline. She remembered how she had never been so afraid as she tried to keep the children calm. Two forts had been set up. One was on Roanoke Island; the north end area is where the army camp was located. The other was in what is known as Bowsertown in Manteo, NC. The area was mostly woodland, which led to the sound. "This is where the Germans had made camp," she said in the interview.

She lived right in between the two forts, only miles apart. She said the aircraft flying came right over her house so low at the time. She could feel the earth shake, she said. Sometimes things would fall over in the house from the shaking. This went on for days. She described how the Germans were captured right back there in Bowsertown. Bowsertown is within walking distance of her home. She laughed, saying, "We knew they would come to get them. We know something was happening with all the aircraft flying. More cannonballs were being dropped than we had ever heard, and we could hear the cannonballs whistling over the house. Afraid, the family huddled together, praying until it was over," she told me in the interview.

The men in the community went out to look around after the war was over. They soon came back to get shovels to dig holes to bury the many bodies they had to find on the shore and in the sound of floating. "The bodies were floating clear around Burnside," she said. The children were told not to go back there, but children being children, they would sneak off and go anyway. It was nothing to go back there and find cannonballs, and she was unsure whether it would explode. Sometimes, they would find coins and other things that would wash to shore.

When she was growing up, they had little. You wore clothes from the older children. If your shoes had a hold in the bottom, cardboard was placed inside to cover the hole. It was traditional for the older women to teach the younger women to cook, sew, and do other things they needed to know about life. She talked about a time when people could not find bread or sugar and needed a ration ticket to buy food before and after the war.

Granny's Tillett Scarborough roots are deep in religion, passed down to her from her parents, which she passed down to her children. She told me her life had been blessed with a good husband. His name was Thomas Scarborough, a gifted carpenter in his day. In their marriage, they had seven children Alphonse, Carrie, Arounia, Maloyd, Emerson, Lillian, and Margarette. Granny had a grandson named Robert Wise, born in 1917 and dying in 1945 at age twenty-seven. Robert served his country with North Carolina Pvt. Med. Det. 371 infantry during World War ll. Robert was the son of John Frank Wise and Carrie. Her son, Maloyd, served at the Pea Island all-black lifesaving station. After it closed, Maloyd joined the United States Coast Guard. Arounia was married to Maxie Berry Sr., the son of Joseph Hall Berry; both were keepers at Pea Island. The men who worked there also ate and slept there. It would be months before the men could come home for a week off. When Maxie came home, Arounia would cook his favorite meals; her homemade pineapple cakes were much enjoyed. She would have the whole family gather at her house to see him off; it seemed like a holiday. The Berry family served in the United States Coast Guard for over one hundred years. Granny was proud of her family and loved them all very much, and her family adored her. Her daughter, Margarette, took care of Granny until she passed away at age one hundred.

CHAPTER 5

THE FREEDMEN'S COLONY

The Role Religion and Education Played in the Colony

Religion played a vital protection role in our ancestors' lives. They endured struggles and hardships to hold on to their faith in God. The people know that only God's grace and mercy would get them through away the pain and suffering. To the runaway slaves, Roanoke Island, NC, became known as the Island of Hope. If they could make it over the creek to the Union Army, they would find a haven, a place to start a new life for themselves, prosperity for their families, and most of all, a future for their children.

The first thing they did was find a place to have church services. Out in the woods, they found a clearing of pine trees, where they raised their hands to praise the Lord and sang hymns like "Still Away" and "Nobody Knows the Troubles I've Seen."

The first church was built near Fort Foster. They named the church Haven Creek. In 1862, Union Forces became a haven for African families throughout the region. A Freedmen's Colony was established by the Union Army on the north end of Roanoke Island.

The Union gave the people the first taste of independence and freedom. In March 1862, Congress passed an article of war forbidding Union soldiers from returning fugitive slaves to their owners. The Union Army gave land to the Freedmen's Colony to build homes to live in, a church to worship, a school to teach the children, and a library for the adults to read and write.

Freedmen recruited from Roanoke Island formed the first company of the North Carolina Colored Volunteers. About four thousand North Carolina men enlisted, and more than 150 men were recruited from the Roanoke Island community. The Union Army allowed families of the Freedmen Colony soldiers to live at Roanoke Island as a place of refuge during the war. By the end of the war, there were three thousand to four thousand Freedmen living in the colony. True heroes of their time overcame great obstacles and made significant contributions. They played important roles in world history.

Education was important to the Freedmen Colony. In 1863, Miss Elizabeth James was the first teacher sent out by the American Missionary Association. She and others came to teach the Freedmen community. As the colony grew, several more schools were built. Seven teachers came to the colony to teach; the horrifying living conditions broke their hearts, giving the teachers more compassion for the Freedmen people. The teachers did all they could to teach the eager children and adults to read and write.

The Freedmen women were knowledgeable of herbal remedies, which were often more effective than what doctors could offer. The condition in the colony had become crowded, bringing infectious diseases to the people. What the colony had to go through was pitiable, living in shack houses with no running water, oil lamps to see at night or food. They prayed morning and night for deliverance. In time, life for African people somewhat improved.

"As a young girl, I remember an old lady who lived on Manteo Airport Road. The old-timers talked about how she had come from the Freedmen's Colony. She never left the house she lived in. I don't know her name, but I believe she lived to be over 105 years old."

After the war ended in 1865, government orders stated that all land confiscated by the Union Army must be returned to the former owners if they could find a title to the land. The churches that the Freedmen had built were still allowed to use. In 1879, John B. Etheridge and his wife, Fannie, deeded it to Richard Etheridge, John Woodly, Edward Wise, and Dempsey Baum on July 7, 1879 (deed book A, page 407, in Dare County Register of Deeds office).

As time passed, people started to live on the island. Most of the people moved all around the country, trying to find a better life. At that time, African Americans could buy land for around four hundred dollars.

It's unclear what happened to the Freedmen's church or why the members stopped going. Maybe after relocating, it was beyond walking distance. The members built a second church, located on Burnside Road; it became home to Haven Creek church, built around 1887. Another church was built there in 1914. The church was destroyed by a storm in 1944. Today, it is the Haven Creek Baptist Cemetery. The present-day church is on Sir Walter Raleigh Street in Manteo, NC. It has the same name today as Haven Creek Missionary Baptist Church.

Now, free citizens, and ex-slaves contributed to the United States. If not for the slave labor of the Freedmen's Colony, North Carolina wouldn't be as beautiful as it is today. The people demonstrated bravery and perseverance as they found their freedom. "The struggles of our people should always be remembered and taught to our children. Otherwise, they will not know how integration came about and how our ancestors paved the way for us so the road would be a little smoother. Our youth should know things don't come without a struggle."

The Freedmen had to fight to get their freedom from the cotton fields to having to sit on the back of the bus or going to a little window on the side or back of a building to buy anything. The people couldn't vote or have a say in their future. "When we look back at these days, yes, we have come a long way, but we still have a long way to go—especially in this day and time, when there is so much hate and new Jim Crow laws are being brought to the land to hold back black lives."

All opportunities come through struggle, even though the grievances are numerous. African Americans and white people should work together to ensure equal opportunity for all people. The Freedmen Colony was born into the movement. We need to understand the sacrifices the movement requires of those who came before us. Do we know how far back the movement goes? All I know is we can't ever stop the movement. We have a rich history in Dare County, NC. Residents recall stories of their ancestors, descendants of the Freedmen Colony, with names such as Midgett, Pugh, Baum, Wise, Daniels, Tillett, Etheridge, Bowser, Scarborough, Collins, and Simmons.

This chapter was written by my mother, Dellerva Wise Collins, called Dell, who passed away in 2005. It comprises speeches she made at church and during Black History Month. You will read more about Dell in the chapters to come.

CHAPTER 6

A YOUNG MAN'S LIFE
AFTER WORLD WAR 1

John Frank Wise

John Frank Wise was born on December 28, 1872. A 1920 census shows his draft registration card for World War l. John had a son, Robert Wise, who died serving during World War ll. He also had two sisters, Cora Wise McClease and Sabra A. Wise appeared on an 1880 census when Sabra was three years old. John Frank married Edna Bowser Wise (you read about her family and John Frank in chapter 3). They had six children: Hattie, John Grant, Sabra, Stanley, Elwood, and Dellerva.

When John was seven, his mother left John here on the island with his father's family. She went up north to work in a factory. She would send money back home to the family, which cared for John and his sisters. Without their mother, life was hard for John and his sisters. The people they lived with were unkind to the children. As a young boy, John would have many chores.

John Frank's grandmother and grandfather came to Roanoke Island's Freedmen's colony to find their freedom. It is unknown where they came from, but it is believed they may have come from West Africa. John's father was an experienced cobbler; his handcrafting skills came from Africa and Ethiopia.

Shortly after John and Edna were married, John was drafted off to war. John didn't want to leave home, but he had to go. Edna, along with other Wise family members worked on a farm owned by Claude Esley (born in 1881, died in 1956) and his wife, Bertha Meekins Wise. This is where the African American Wise family of Manteo, NC, derives. The family worked on the farm for many years. After Claude passed, one of his sons took over the farm. His name was Robert Wills Wise (born in 1922, died in 2007). According to the story, the white family was mean and treated the African Americans like second-class citizens, calling them deplorable names and paying them little to nothing.

While serving in the war, John Frank was met with the horrible conflicts of war. John was wounded when struck by a mini-ball in his leg, which had to be amputated. When John got well, he came back wearing a wooden leg. Historians have estimated that just under thirty thousand Union soldiers lost a limb during the war. When John returned home, Edna took good care of him as he continued to recover. John would tell Edna she had healing hands. He would ask her to touch his aching leg because it made it feel better.

Edna played an essential role in human health. If you got sick, she made you better using herbal and plant remedies. Her techniques had been passed down to her by her mother and grandmother. She became a Red Cross Volunteer, helping to save lives. She was soft-spoken and very caring of others. If you needed food, she would feed you. If you had nowhere to stay, she would give you a place to sleep. In her time, people looked out for each other. This was a part of her upbringing, which she passed down to her family. The characteristic she possessed is what John Frank admired about Edna.

After his recovery, he and his wife returned to work in his shoe shop. As they worked, they would have the children with them. The children would play around with their father's shoe block as he worked. So he would give them nails to hammer into the shoe block. The children's nails are still in the block. The shoe block has been in the Wise-Collins family for more than one hundred years. You can see John Frank and his shoe block on the back of this book.

The stories our grandmother told showed us what a hero he was to his family as a husband, father and grandfather—the love they had for each other, the pain and heartache they endured, which no one will ever really know. In those days, people of African or Indian descent had to be careful in their day-to-day lives to travel where they needed to be. Edna would tell stories about how they would ensure they were back in the house before dark. People were being lynched on what was called Lucy's Corner. Today, it is the site of the

Pea Island Cookhouse, in Collins Park, named after John Frank and Edna's daughter, Dellerva Wise Collins.

John Frank and Edna purchased property on what is now Sir Walter Raleigh Extension, which their family owns today. This is where our family legacy began. We do not know much about John Frank. What we do know is a part of rich American history, which, although painful, makes us all proud they all made it when so many others did not.

CHAPTER 7

A PROFILE OF AFRICAN AMERICANS IN DARE COUNTY

Past and Present

Richard Pigford was born in 1859 in Burgaw, NC. He was a runaway slave and ended up here with the Freedmen Colony. He married a Manteo lady, Martha Meekins, the sister of Theodore Meekins. After Richard's service with the all-African American crew at the Pea Island Life Saving, he was a brave man who enjoyed farming and fishing. He died in 1921. James Creecy Daniels and Sadie Daniels King were his grandchildren.

William "Wille" Simmons served at Pea Island, after which he retired on disability. His ancestors came here to the Freedmen's Colony. He married a local girl, Arnetta Berry, Joseph Berry's daughter. After his retirement, he kept a beautiful farm. In the early 1970s, he was appointed to the Manteo Board of Commissioners. His descendants still live on the land today.

W. C. Bowser was born in 1849 as a free man on Roanoke Island and lived at Butts Swamp. He resigned from Pea Island and became a boat builder.

William S. Bowser, son of W. C. Bowser, was born in 1881 and also served at Pea Island. He lived on Roanoke Island and retired in 1922. He later became an insurance agent. He still has relatives living on the island today.

George R. Midgett was born in 1839 on the Outer Banks of North Carolina as a slave. He was a soldier in the Civil War and later served at Pea Island. After service, he served as a judge and built a windmill for grinding grain. If it wasn't for the Midgett family, Dare County could have starved. George also built his fishing boat out of a pine tree. He has descendants living here today.

Joseph H. Berry was born in 1873 on Roanoke Island. His mother, Mary Baum, was a slave. His home was at the causeway in Manteo, NC. Joseph, his son, and his grandson all served at Pea Island. A host of grandsons served and continue to serve in the United States Coast Guard. After his retirement, he framed and fished until he became physically disabled.

John Pigford the son of Richard and Martha Pigford. John served as the first Civil Defense leader for Dare County.

George Pruden was born in 1887. His mother, Catherina Pruden, came here to the Freedmen's Colony and later married Henry Woodley. She was a well-known midwife. One night, she delivered two babies on the same night within minutes of the two women, who lived a good distance apart.

Heartwarmingly, everyone called her Puss. Sarah Baxter was also a midwife in Dare County.

Robert T. "Bob" Bowser, whose birth is unknown, operated an oyster-shucking house east of Elizabeth II, in the Town of Manteo, NC, in the early 1900s.

The late Evelyn Midgett Wescott was born in 1909. She was a seamstress for WPA. Her father, George Harvey Midgett, was born in 1879, and her grandfather, George Riley Midgett, was born in 1838. The family-owned property sat on Highway 64/264 in Manteo, located on the land was the only windmill on the island, which was used to grind cornmeal for food and other products for Dare County residents.

Richard Etheridge, the first black commander of the all-black Pea Island Lifesaving Station, is buried with his family on the grounds of the North Carolina Aquarium.

Maxie Berry was born in 1898 to Joseph Hall Berry and Angenora Pugh Berry. He was the last commander of the all-black Pea Island Lifesaving Station. He was a BMC United States Coast Guard, Ret., World War I and II.

Eva Armstrong Bethea was born in 1905. She was from Elizabeth City, NC, and came to Manteo to teach at the all-black school. After integration, Mrs. Bethea was hired to teach in the Dare County public school system. She taught at Manteo Elementary until she retired. Ella Dundor, Cavin Tillett,

Oscar Woodley, and Sylvia Mackey were the first local teachers in Dare County.

Robert Tillett and Johnson Ashby were boat captains. They charged a small fee and some time for a trade of goods for a day of fishing in the sound around Roanoke Island, NC. Robert Tillett, using his boat, delivered mail from the Manteo docks to Frisco.

Thomas T. Scarborough was born in 1875. As a first-class carpenter, he built the old Martin Johnson home, once owned by the captain of Trenton, which made daily trips to Elizabeth City, NC, and back to the island.

John Ebron operated a cleaning and pressing business in Dare County. At the time, they were located on the site of the Balfour Baum home.

Malinda Tillett's date of birth is unknown to the writer. Malinda cooked meals for the officers at Fort Burnside during the Civil War.

Elder George J. McClease Sr. was born in 1922. He brought the first insurance agency to African Americans in Dare County, which was necessary because white people wouldn't sell insurance to them. It is known as the Brother's Aid Society. He became the president. His wife Pinnie, his children, and his grandchildren live here on the island.

Marshall Collins born 1898 operated a crab-picking business located northeast of the old courthouse in Downtown Manteo, NC.

Lila Simmons was born in 1894. In her days, she was a first-class quilter and pillow maker for the residents of Dare County.

Dare County's first four African American schools were located (1) in what was now Manteo Airport on Airport Road (2) in the area of Burnside Road, (3) at the intersection en route to the beach, and (4) where the Roanoke Community Center was located. Dare County was integrated in 1964.

PFC William Seward Simmions Jr. served our country as a member of the United States Army. On August 1, 1967, in South Vietnam, at the age of nineteen, he lost his life. The brave young man should always be remembered. William's name is on the panel of the Vietnam Memorial Wall in Washington, DC. He is the son of William Seward and Earlene Simmons.

Thomas Scarborough, Ida Davenport, Nora Berry, Bethanie Tillett, and Cloudie M. Blackmond were born and raised in Hatteras, NC.

Graham Edward Spencer, the husband of Ada Beatrice Scarborough Spencer, was born in 1873. The couple contributed to their community by donating the property to the church, a place where their community still has a place to worship: Heaven Creek Missionary Baptist Church, on Sir Walter Raleigh Street in Manteo, NC.

James Melvin has loved art since he was a little boy, learning from his father. His success and dreams are within his religious beliefs. James is an artist and owner of Malvin's Studio in Nags Head, NC. James is an illustrator for writers, including children's book author Suzanne Tate's *Nature* series. He is the artist of the *Pea Island Lifesavers* series, at the North Carolina Aquarium, in Manteo. He is on the board of directors of the Dare County Art Council and much more.

Beulah Charity Ashby, retired office manager for Dare County Water Department, is the daughter of the late Raymond and Ada Pearl Spencer Charity. Beulah's mother named called Pearl. Pearl was the daughter of the late Graham and Ada Scarborough Spencer. Pearl's mother's origins are rooted in Middletown, Hyde County, NC. Ada is the daughter of Celia Jane Collins Scarborough. Celia's parents were John and Billy Ann Barber Collins.

Pearl was a strong fighter in the Civil Rights Movement. She had nine children, and she fought hard for the future of her family and community. She attended the boycott of the Hyde County schools. The community was concerned for Pearl's safety. No one wanted anything bad to happen to Pearl, so family and friends prayed to keep her safe from all the terror and danger. When she told everyone who she would be going with, everyone strongly sensed that Pearl would be fine—because of the two private bodyguards she traveled with to Hyde County. The two men were among the most formidable in the African American community. Dorn Washington was known as "Ram Gully," and Otis Pledger was known as "Crow." Pearl was with the A-Team. There was no doubt she would make it to the march and back home safely, and she did.

Tonya L. Collins, professional broker and owner of Outer Banks Dreams Realty, helped families find their dream homes, one at a time. She was the wife of Darrell Collins, historian, and member of the Town of Manteo Commissioners Board.

Sharon Golden was a secretary for the Dare County Administration Office. She left to join the United States Army, where she made it her career. Sharon served in the Iraq War, which lasted from 2003 to 2011. Noah McClease and Keith Bowser also served in the Iraq war.

Jacqueline "Jackie" Tillett has been a secretary for the Dare County Planning Department. Jackie has had many challenging duties, which she always handled with professionalism. On August 19, 2020, Jackie was named elections director for the county. Jackie is the daughter of the late William Leo Tillett Jr. and Dorothy "Dot" Tillett.

The only shoe repairman in Dare County was John Frank Wise, the father of Dell Wise Collins. After his death, his wife, Edna Wise, continued the trade until a shop opened in the Town of Manteo.

Joseph "Joe" Tillett was a large-scale farmer for Dare County and sold his plants and produce to local stores and residents.

Virginia Simmons Tillett, by popular vote, served as a member of the Dare County Board of Education, where she became chairperson. Virginia was promoted to assistant dean of Administrative Services at the College of Albemarle. Dare County campus. She was recognized by the governor of North Carolina.

Leon Daniels coached for the Babe Ruth League for thirty years. He served as a petty officer with the United States Coast Guard for twenty-three years. He was a successful businessman, having his own insurance company, Leon Daniels Enterprises Seaway, in Kill Devils Hill, NC.

Organic Mechanic Landscaping, LLC, has many years of experience in Architectural and Engineering Services, working in Manteo and the surrounding towns and villages of North Carolina. The company was founded by Norfleet Daniels. Norfleet has continued to grow his company, taking great pride in his work.

Ralph Berry comes from a long line of the Berry family legacy in the Coast Guard, making history in the United States Coast Guard as the first African American to become a scuba diver.

Arvilla Tillett Bowser and her husband, Lindsey Bowser, are the authors of *Roanoke Island: The Forgotten Colony*. Arvilla is the granddaughter of Joseph "Joe" Tillett.

Rev. Calvin Moore served as chairman of the Department of Social Services Board. He was appointed to serve as magistrate for Dare County. His wife, Lovey Burton Moore, was director of a major federal program, with a branch in Dare County Head Start. Her sister, Gloria Burton, has a son, Steven Burton, Dare County's first African American semi-pro baseball player.

Carol Scott is a white woman who had a heart of gold. She saw no color when it came to our history or people. Her research of Roanoke Island brought the history of the Underground Railroad to Roanoke Island. Carol, Eugene

Austin, and Dellerva Collins traveled to Ohio to the National Park Service Regional Office to negotiate the story of Harriet Tubman, who brought slaves to freedom here on Roanoke Island. The meeting was set up by Carol, who started the negotiations. The meeting took a turn for the worse, with no possibility of success, after Carol became frustrated with the uncertainty of the man's ineptitude. Dell had been listening quietly when she stepped in. She told me that she didn't even know what she had said to the man, but she knew God was a part of that day. After she spoke to the man, he decided to rule in their favor.

Gina Owens of Gina's Art Studio is a local artist known for her paintings of colorful island fish. Her artwork can be seen throughout the county.

Andreas Etheridge received a Registered Nursing degree in 2021. This had not been accomplished in Dare County's African American community in over forty years. Congratulations, Andreas. Son of Marcia and Donald Etheridge, Donald is the owner of Duck N Sons Detailing, in Manteo, NC.

Some of Dare County's best professional chefs in the community were William "Baby" Cross, Ada Pearl Charity, James Overton, Hilda Davenport, Annie Mae Daniels, Lula Tillett, Elaine Peterson, Lillian Austin, Bessie Mae Farrow, Dorothy Drake, Audrey Mae Charity, Mabel Burton Porter, Beulah Daniels, Milton Selby, Milton Jerome Selby, Alvin Selby, Geraldine Davenport Moore, Merium Darmon Collins, Earlene Bryant Simmons, Cora Tillett Scarborough, Margaret Wise, Charlie and Gloria White Pledger, and Edna

Wise. It also includes the King of Pig Roasting, Calvin Carver, and wild game chefs Anthony "Tony" Green and Donnie Murray.

Denise "Necy" Morris Howard has made history in Dare County by becoming the first African American to operate a business in Downtown Manteo in over one hundred years. "Go, Necy, go." Look for Necy at Necy's Baby Cakes in Downtown Manteo.

Ozella Scarborough was an expert in quiltmaking. During her time in history, it was a tradition for women to make quilts for their families. The only way for people to heat their homes was with a wood stove. When the stove burned out in the middle of the night, you were thankful for those big, heavy quilts (although you needed help to get them off you). She was the last in the African American community to make this type of handmade quilt. She was a sweet, kind, loving, and fun person to be with. Her wisdom always gave young people encouragement. Her deep love for her family and friends will always be remembered and appreciated.

Eula Bell Eborn Mackey was the coordinator of Senior Nutrition Services. The program is in partnership with the Albemarle Commission. The program provides adults sixty and older with nutritious meals five days a week. Eula was employed by the Green Thumb program, which provides income-eligible senior citizens with part-time employment in the state agencies through the not-for-profit Beautification, Inc, enacted by the state legislature in 1974. Mildred Spencer Ebron also worked for Green Thumb. She worked for the

Economic Improvement Council as assistant to Dell Collins Community Coordinator for all of Dare County. Mildred was partially blind and a member of the Lions Club for the Blind.

Each spring, Ludie Belle Ebron Sykes participated in the Outer Banks Senior Games. The mission is to promote healthy active lifestyles for seniors. It is unclear how many years she attended, but in her nineties, her athletic career bloomed. Her achievement is recognized with gold, silver, and bronze awards. Ludie won eleven or more gold medals in the years she participated in the Senior Games. She enjoyed pickleball, softball throw, and the silver strider's fun walk. Ludie lived to be 103.

Naomi Collins Hester was a PE teacher at Manteo High School. She was appointed to the Board of Trustees for Elizabeth City State University. She worked for the Dare County Board of Education until she retired. She is the daughter of Marshall and Gussie Collins. Her husband, Osborn Hester, was president of the Manteo Fire Department.

Tshombe Selby was born in 1983 to the late Milton "Jerome" Selby and Barbara Jean Drake Selby. Tshombe's family roots are deeply embedded in Dare County. He also has deep roots in Hyde County, NC, where his father was from. The foundation was built on spiritual faith, courage, musical talents, and love for self and others. Tshombe has all these characteristics; he is the third-generation grandson of the famous Theodore M. Meekins. Tshombe is a rising star in classical music. He lives in New York and plays with the

Metropolitan Opera House. Terence Blanchard reopened the 138-year-old Opera Company as the first African American composer. Tshombe was a part of the performance as a character in "Fire Shut Up in My Bones." His family and friends in Dare and Hyde County are proud of Tshombe. He is on his way to becoming famous.

Ruth Bowser Lewis is a native of Dare County. She is the daughter of Hazel Pearl Bowser Scarborough and her father, Lloyd Meekins Sr. His brother is Theodore Meekins, and her husband is Clarence Lewis. She is a mother of six. Ruth introduces the Economic Improvement Council to Dare County, which is still servicing the county. She was the first African American to work for the Dare County Department of Social Services, as a social worker.

Doris Creecy, a native of Wilmington, NC, taught in Fayetteville schools, including Norfolk State University. She is a retired fourth-grade schoolteacher at Manteo Elementary school and the founder and director of a local singing group. The Echo of Heritage is a group that sings a cappella old Negro spiritual hymns, including "Wade in the Water," "Swing Low, Sweet Chariot," "Steal Away," "Amazing Grace," and many more. Through her musical talent, she honors our ancestor's roots in slavery.

Vanzolla McMurran is recognized for her hard work with the Dare County Register of Deeds Office. Vanzolla has over thirty years of experience, with no hidden agendas. She served several years as the assistant before moving up to the Register of Deeds, receiving a plurality of the votes cast. She worked diligently for the people of Dare County.

Aquilla Burton Bryant and Priscilla Burton Hardy are twins (not the only twins born in the African American community in Dare County). The two have lived in the community for over seventy years. The ladies have always had words of inspiration for the youth of the community. God has always made way for the two of them to be there for families, friends, and anyone who might need a helping hand. They are an example of what African American family unity should look like. The community is blessed to have two such loving and caring people.

Yolanda Collins, Catherine Bowser, and Deborah Burton were regulated state license home preschools in the African American community for over thirty years. The three of them are highly respected. At the time, Mamie Morris McMurran was headteacher at Head Start. Mamie and Yolanda earned a CDA (child development associate) degree, the equivalent of an associate's degree. The two were the only providers in the county to pass the course. Between the four, the women have over fifty successful years improving the lives of children and families in Dare County. Dell Collins was always there for all of us, providing friendly advice when needed. Gloria Burton and Ethel Burton Bowser also had a center.

Gladys Melvin was a registered nurse. She worked with the Dare County Health Department, one of the best in the county. She taught nursing courses at Manteo College of Albemarle. Gladys had strong religious beliefs, with a love for everyone.

Kaleta Daniels Govan served as a bookkeeper for Child Nutrition in the Dare County Board of Education.

The Golden Age Club was the first senior group to be organized in Dare County. At the time, the effort of Pat Fearing was associated with the Economic Improvement Council. Dell Collins became an organizer and advisor to the first group of seniors from the African American community. Some of the seniors were born in the 1800s and early 1900s. The people were George Midgett, Lila Simmons, Harriet Ashby, Eunice Scarborough, Odessa Meekins, Elizabeth Barber, Maulsie Phillips, Agatha Gray, Edna Wise, Arnetta Simmons, Myrtle Scarborough, Sallie Jane Scarborough, Arounia Berry, Mildred Ebron, Earlene Simmons, Elsie Daniels, Willam Cross, Lillian Cross, and Lizzy Farrow. The group was first recognized from May 15 to May 20, 1972, for their arts and crafts display at the Southgate Mall in Elizabeth City, NC. The group took a trip to tour Washington, DC, in the spring, when the cherry trees were blooming. Dell keeps the group busy doing things. One special event for the seniors was a talent and fashion show lunch. The seniors put on a show and had a blast. Each month, the group would celebrate members' birthdays with cake and ice cream. Dell worked with the seniors until her death. Dell loved her seniors, and the seniors loved Dell.

Cassie Lee Cole is a retired registered nurse. She worked at the Albemarle Hospital her entire career. She helped take care of many Dare County residents that had to be admitted. And a lot of the time, patients would ask for Cassie to be their nurse. Cassie has dedicated her life to caring for others. She has always put God first in her life and has shown her love for others. Her life has been blessed with a wonderful husband and two children. Cassie is the great-granddaughter of Theodore Meekins of the all-black Pea Island life-saving service.

Izetta Bowser Redmon was the first African American born in Wanchese, NC, to William Spencer Bowser and Izetta Ross Hopkins. Izetta was a retired teacher and enjoyed fishing on the Outer Banks. Izetta lived in Elizabeth City, NC.

Thaddeus Arnell "Thad" Pledger Sr. was the chief of the Southern Shores Police Department. He was born in 1962 and ascended to his heavenly home in 2006. Thaddeus was a humble, confident, well-dressed gentleman. He took pride in his accomplishments and displayed leadership by offering kindness to others.

Fort Burnside was built by Dare County African American residents. Maloyd Berry organized the Dare County NAACP. Betty Selby serves as president; she also is a member of the Town of Manteo Commissioners and serves as mayor pro tem.

The Dare County Department of Social Service was the first agency in Dare County to hire an African American in a professional area.

Thelma Meekins Thrash is the daughter of the late Lloyd L. Meekins Sr. and Janie Mae Collins Meekins. Thelma was a professional hairdresser. She could press your hair so good it would be like silk. Back then, it was the hot comb method that was placed on heat and also one to curl your hair. Her curls would last a month or until you washed your hair again. Thelma invented the mobile hair salon, where she would put the things she needed to do one's hair in the back of her car. Thelma would wash, press, and curl her clients' hair at their homes.

Dellerva Wise Collins was the first woman to work as a salesperson in the Fearing's Department store in 1967. She was county coordinator for the Economic Improvement Council. She was elected by popular vote as Manteo Town Commissioner and Mayor Pro Tem in 1979. Dell challenged an election on write-in votes, took it to the Courts of Appeal, and won. It made changes in the law on how to do a write-in vote. It is in the legal reference book as *Collins v. Midgett.* Her son, Darrell Collins, retired as a National Park Service Wright Brothers historian. He still travels all over the country to tell the story of Orville and Wilbur Wright. Deborah Tillett was Miss Dare County in 1972. She is the niece of Dell Collins.

You are welcome to visit Manteo to see the historic African American community. At Cartwright Park, on the corner of Sir Walter Raleigh Extension and Bideford Street in Manteo, NC. There at the park are the ruins of the First AME Zion Church, which is known as the Mother Church. Andrew Cartwright was a minister and an agent of the American Colonization Society. He moved to Manteo and established the first African Methodist Episcopal Church, here in 1865. The ruin has been lifted on Roanoke Island by God for the world to see.

After the Civil War, he preached to the people from the Freedmen's Colony. At one time, the church was the only one in the community, and it was still used in the early 1900s. Stories have been told about how the church would be packed, with people who had come from everywhere. The old-timers said the preachers were the best they had ever heard, and there, many camp meetings were held outside. Some preachers came from Africa along with Andrew on his travels to and from the island. They weren't radicals but came to offer help to the people so they might survive, letting them know God was on their side and a brighter day would come. They preached about the sins of slavery and prayed about the wrongs committed against them, telling the people to find work, save their money, and buy land to build a home. The preachers came with words of encouragement.

They preached about freedom and its importance in their lives. At the time, any little thing could cost them their freedom. Losing their freedom meant being punished by being put on a chain gang or road gang (a group of prisoners chained together). The men and women were Africans, our first ancestors. During the 1960s, driving through Currituck, NC, one saw chain gangs on the side of the road, digging ditches. North Carolina used the chain gang into the 1970s. The prisoners worked as free labor to build and construct white corporate America. Men sought to escape the dangerous and unpleasant treatment.

African Americans have always been a target. What did we do to anyone? What did our ancestors do? We are all of the human race, brothers, and sisters in Christ. The African American community has sorrowfully endured being the victim of power. The preachers who came to Manteo brought a beacon of light for the people.

The African Methodist Episcopal Zion Church is a historically African American Christian denomination, based in the United States since the 1700s. Back then, laws prohibited blacks from preaching. This didn't stop the people from searching for their religious freedoms, and AME churches were built all over North Carolina.

A church family from AME Zion would visit the site in Manteo for several years before it became Cartwright Park, not sure where the people had come from. The people would spend the day in fellowship and have lunch. They brought their tables, chairs, coolers, and food for lunch. This was done in honor of those who had come before them.

It was Dell Collins's pleasure to have met those wonderful people. This was the start of the park in the African American Community. She looked forward to seeing them each year they came back to visit.

Dell had made friendships with some of the people. An old man—Mr. James, I believe—invited Dell to bring her children to Wilmington, NC, telling her Wilmington knew a great deal of untold black history. He said our children should know their history and it was important to their futures.

We visited Mr. James and met him at a small café for lunch. After leaving the café, he took us on a ride past the boat dock, big old buildings, the railroad track, and the graveyard. We found it strange that he drove his car in front of us as we followed him, not stopping as he drove around town. As we prepared to leave, he asked if we could come to his house, as he had one more thing to show us. His home was well kept. We sat at his kitchen table and marveled at the large windows all around the kitchen. He was walking around, looking out all his windows to see if anyone might have been listening. Times had not changed that much, he said.

"Some of our history they don't want us to talk about. If the wrong person hears you, something just might happen to you," he said.

He talked about his family, killed in the massacre of the African American community in Wilmington, NC. He told us about the railroad track he had shown us, how it was used to tie African Americans to the track and run trains over them, how the empty old buildings were once black-owned businesses and how a group of white people killed more than six thousand people.

For many years, he said, there were sightings of an old African man with a lit lantern, walking down the middle of the railroad tracks. As a young boy, he and his friends were curious about this story. They would go down to the track at night, trying to see what it was. Most of the time, they would get scared and run. He said if they got too close, it would disappear. He told us he believed it to be the restless souls of his and other African American Ancestors of Wilmington, NC.

African Americans know all too well about the hardships endured by our people then and now, including all the senseless deaths each day among ourselves or at the hand of the police. The African American communities need more funding, better jobs with better pay, better education, and decent housing. This is true if you live in a small county town or a large city, like those in Florida, where a young boy named Trayvon Martin was a target of power, gunned down in his neighborhood. No justice has ever been served.

In New York, Eric Garner died from an illegal chokehold. Breonna Taylor, from Louisville, Kentucky, was shot and killed in her apartment as she slept. It was later discovered the officers had the wrong apartment. Philando Castile of St. Paul, Minnesota, was shot and killed in his car along with his fiancé and young daughter.

George Floyd was murdered by a police offer in Minneapolis, Minnesota.

George was born in Fayetteville, NC. Remember the words of his little daughter: "My daddy changes the world." Andrew Brown was shot and killed by Elizabeth City Sheriffs' Office Deputies, serving an arrest and search warrant. Let's talk about black-on-black crimes, at a critical level all across America. Poverty is a more direct link to these types of crimes than any other factor. The poverty rate is more than twice as high among African Americans as among whites. This is due to four hundred years of systematic racism more than anything else. The lives of innocent men, women, and children are being lost. Dare County has felt the pain of these senseless murders. One of our own, Takeyia De'Shay Berry, age thirty-nine, and her precious baby girl, Allura Monae Pledger, age three, are among these victims. Let's always remember these two beautiful lives. Many, many more black lives across the nation could be named.

So many deaths of people from all around the United States. We may not have had a personal connection to any of the precious souls, but our connection is that we are also living this threat. Therefore, it affects all African American communities. By the 1980s, the stage was being set to destroy African American communities. It wasn't a war on drugs; it was a war to oppress African Americans. This was when black communities all over the nation started to fall apart. There were no resources for the African American communities, only an invasion of a new drug that destroyed lives. This played a part in the long list of black lives murdered by hands meant to protect us.

In the 1980s, it was a small station of the Trailways Bus Company, in Dare County. The bus was never crowded until the day a group of forty or more people got off. The people came into the African American community and started handing out crack cocaine like peppermint candy. Our community is still feeling the impact of the destruction.

In the 1990s, the "Tough on Crime" movement became a school-to-prison pipeline. Another reconstructive form of law is to keep people of color in bondage. African American men and women of Dare County have been caught up in this pipeline, and some are still incarcerated. Our community has been affected by children taken away from their families, their lives lost. What a price to pay for something that was planted in communities all across America. At this time, Dellerva "Dell" Collins was a one-woman team, a warrior for the African American community of Dare County. She would run people selling drugs out of Cartwright Park and the corner, telling them about the church there in the park.

"Boys," she would say, "if you got this gift of salesmanship, why not become a car dealer or sell some T-shirts and caps? Have pride in your community. If you see a piece of trash on the ground, pick it up. Don't let strangers come into your community and take over. This is an African American community, rich in history, and should always be known as Dare County's African American community."

Dell's family and friends would tell Dell to stay out of the corner before someone hurt her. She had a way of talking to them, and they always gave her respect. She cleaned up the corner. Our love is what our ancestors had, which no one could take from us. Because of love, we have survived.

What did we do?

CHAPTER 8

THE FIRST AFRICAN AMERICANS PATHFINDERS IN PUBLIC SERVICE, THE 1800S–2022

Mary McLean Bethune was named Director of Negro Affairs of National Youth Administration on June 24, 1936, and received a major United States government appointment.

Frederick Douglass was named United States marshal of the District of Columbia on March 18, 1877.

The first black man in Congress and the first black United States Senator, Hiram R. Revels, of Mississippi, was seated on February 25, 1870.

Shirley Chisholm was elected to the Ninety-First District. Winning the seat for Brooklyn on November 5, 1968, she became the first African American woman in the United States Congress. Her historic run for president shook up the 1972 campaign.

Joseph H. Rainey of South Carolina was seated in the House of Representatives on December 12, 1870.

Carl B. Stokes of Cleveland and Richard G. Hatcher of Gary were inaugurated in the Twentieth Century around 1967 as mayors of major American cities.

Robert C. Weaver, a cabinet member, was named secretary of the Department of Housing Development by President Lyndon B. Johnson. He was sworn in on January 18, 1966.

Patricia R. Harris, a cabinet member, was appointed to the Department of Housing and Urban Development by President Jimmy Carter on December 21, 1976. She was also an ambassador serving in Luxembourg.

Judge William H. Heastie was confirmed as a judge of the Federal District Court of the Virgin Islands on March 26, 1937.

James B. Parsons was named to the Federal District Courts of Northern Illinois on August 9, 1961, by President John F. Kennedy.

In 2001, Condoleezza Rice was appointed national security adviser by President George W. Bush. She became the first African American woman (or any woman) to hold the post. Condoleezza also served as the US secretary of state as the first African American.

Barack Hussein Obama served two terms as the Forty-Fourth president of the United States. From 2009 to 2017, he served as the first African American president.

Kamala Devi Harris is the first African American woman to serve as vice president of the United States.

Judge Ketanji Brown Jackson was the first African American woman to sit on the Supreme Court. She was appointed by President Joseph "Joe" R. Biden Jr. in April 2022.

CHAPTER 9

SEGREGATION AND INTEGRATION IN PUBLIC SCHOOLS IN EASTERN NORTH CAROLINA

A Fight to Save African American Schools

The National Association for the Advancement of Colored People (NAACP) had long sought strategies to desegregate schools, but it wasn't until *Brown v. Board of Education* in 1954 that the United States Supreme Court outlawed segregation.

During segregation, African American schools received less funding than white schools. Dare County wasn't an exception. The African American school only had three classrooms for first grade to twelfth grade, with overcrowded rooms, inadequate toilets, a lack of supplies, and insufficient pay for teachers.

The students who went to this school recall the struggles of having so little. Teachers made the best of what they did have. Children had to behave, so the teachers were strict and stern. Either you learned, or you had no recess. The school never got anything new; they inherited the things white schools no longer wanted, and most of the time, the items came damaged. The Board of Education would send white high school students to the African American school to back old, torn-up books. The white students would throw the books on the lawn and call them names. After the white students had left, the other students came outside to pick up the books. When the children would attempt to read the books, the middle pages had often been ripped out. Perhaps what might have been meant to harm only expanded their creative thinking, as gifted teachers would have the children create what was missing from the story.

In another story, around the early 1950s, the Board of Education sent a bus to a school to pick up African American students. The entire school was taken, boys and girls, to Elizabeth City, NC, to the Albemarle Hospital. The students thought they were going to the dentist, but instead, they all had their tonsils and adenoids taken out. To this day, people ask, what was this all about? Was it some type of testing on African American students?

As the students got older, parents sent their children away for a better education. Many went to PW Moore High School in Elizabeth City, NC, and others went north.

The Civil Rights Act of 1957 was passed by Congress. In 1957, we had Little Rock, which was frightening to all African Americans. In 1959, four African American men, students at North Carolina Agricultural and Technical College, visited Woolworth in Greensboro, NC. The men sat down at a whites-only lunch counter for coffee. This was the start of Greensboro sit-ins. This protest triggered similar protests in the South. The Freedom Riders happened in 1961, and in 1963, during the march on Washington, DC, nearly 250,000 people attended to hear Dr. King's "I Have a Dream" speech.

Ten years later, the Supreme Court ruled that segregated schools were unconstitutional. Hyde County, NC, remained segregated. When the Hyde County Board of Education was forced to desegregate the schools in 1968, an all-white school board decided to close the historically African American schools.

In 1968, Golden Astro Frinks and other chapters of the Southern Christian Leadership Conference (SCLC), out of New Bern, NC, began a boycott in Hyde County, NC, to desegregate public schools. With the assassination of Dr. Martin Luther King on April 4, 1968, Ralph David Abernathy became president of the National SCLC. He came to Hyde County to support the school's boycott. Abernathy's goal was to demonstrate to the school board that the students and parents had the National SCLC's support of the movement.

In spring 1969, the SCLC had national marches advocating integration in Hyde County, NC. He called for a march from Swan Quarter, NC, to Raleigh, NC. The other was from Asheville, NC, to Raleigh, NC. The goal was to march through as many towns as possible to gain the support of neighboring towns for Hyde County schools.

There was no security for the marchers other than their own members.

Sometimes, as they passed through different towns, the people they met weren't kind. They threw "piss balloons" at the marchers and called them names. When necessary, the marchers would return to the buses they rode to travel through the towns. In other towns, people would be kind, providing hot dogs and water for the marchers and cheering for them. Recalling that dogs and firehoses had been prepared to assault them, they ran.

The African American men would hold meetings to discuss strategies for what to do next. These discussions would be reported to the white community. The Ku Klux Klan started following the African American people, sowing fear. The men knew who was reporting their meetings. Word spread that the KKK was coming to burn the African American community in Engelhard, NC, and other communities were threatened, even in Dare County. The men told the traitor the opposite of what they would do. That night, the men took their shotguns and went to the entrance of their neighborhood, hid in the ditch, and waited. When the Klan came, the men emerged from the ditch with all barrels firing. The Klan didn't know what else to do but run. That night, those brave men saved their community and other towns. People were shot and wounded. The marchers, even little children, were taken to jail. When they were in jail, a racist sheriff intentionally fired tear gas at the protesters. People were hurt jumping out the windows of the jail. They endured a lot. One time, knowing they were going to jail, everyone put a chicken in their pocket. When they got inside, they let the chickens go, and so did the people. Their efforts paid off, as in 1969, citizens of Hyde County voted for a referendum that provided the funding to desegregate the Mattamuskeet school. When talking about the movement to the people that were a part of the march, you could see the teary eyes and heartful pain, which they still feel today. Of all the stories they tell, the most hurtful is that of two young girls, Lucy Howerd and Clara Beckwith, seniors in high school who lost their lives during the movement. Three young high school girls were ambushed by the Klan on their way back to Engelhard from the march in Raleigh. Only one survived. This was a hate crime, and no one was ever punished. To this day, she cannot talk about it much. She did tell me about the large truck that came, with bright lights running them off the road. This happened in Wilson, NC. Somehow, the marchers were trapped. She had to wear a full-body cast for a little over a year. She gives thanks to God and hopes their names will be remembered for generations to come.

Lucy and Clara.

CHAPTER 10

THE VOTING RIGHTS ACT OF 1965

Fighting Together

The Civil Rights Act of 1968

Our Mothers Fight to Vote and Fair Housing for Dare County, Hyde County, and Tyrell County

In the 1950s and 1960s, Jim Crow laws enforced racial segregation in the South. The laws were designed to oppress African Americans in voting, housing, employment, education, and economic prosperity. At the end of Reconstruction and the Civil Rights Movement in the 1950s, African Americans faced discrimination and were mistreated beyond belief. This was a time of horror and turmoil.

"What do we do?" is a question African Americans have asked each other for decades. Jim Crow laws were inhumane. The year 1955 witnessed the lynching of a young fourteen-year-old boy, Emmett Louis Till. All across the country, African American communities were angry and afraid about the brutal condition of the young boy's body. It made people push harder for the Civil Rights Act.

In 1963, after the assassination of the Civil Rights activist Medgar Evers, African Americans protested American department stores. African Americans were urged to withhold their dollars from white corporations, instead donating to African American–led organizations during the holiday season. Stores wouldn't hire African Americans, so a nationwide boycott was held. African Americans were warned not to buy Christmas lights or the Ku Klux Klan would burn down their homes. I remember our mother, Dell, turning the tree lights on during the day and turning them off at night. She was a trailblazer for the civil rights for Dare County's African American community. She had the town of Manteo recognize Martin Luther King Day three years before it became a national holiday.

Two great African American leaders were assassinated: Malcolm X in 1965 and Reverend Dr. Martin Luther King Jr. in 1968. Before them, John F. Kennedy was killed in 1963. In 1965, Americans watched their TVs to the events on that bridge on Bloody Sunday. John Lewis was among the people hurt protesting for the right to vote.

These men were a bedrock of hope for African Americans. With the loss of these strong and courageous men, for a time, life seemed uncertain. It was a scary time for African Americans.

Dare County had white-only and colored-only entrance signs. Stories have been told about how the Pioneer Theater in downtown Manteo had a back entrance for African Americans, where they would sit on a balcony while the white people sat at the bottom. African Americans would throw popcorn, spill drinks, and spit dip juice down on white people. This was their way of getting back at white people for being so hateful to African Americans.

By the mid to late 1960s, African Americans experienced a slight ascent. African American people got jobs they couldn't before. Whites who thought a man of color was moving too fast would try to intimidate him. The Klan would follow African American people coming from work at night. Women trying to make a living for their children would quit their jobs for their safety. A cross was burned in the yard of a prominent African American family. In 1966, the esteemed Lillia Eatella Tillett Boone was hired by the Dare County Board of Education as a high school advanced English teacher. Estella, as she was known, was an activist for political and social change in her community. She would encourage all young African American men to finish school and join the US Coast Guard or other military branches. She knew this would provide opportunities for young men to make a life for themselves and their families. Her death is still a mystery to her family and community. Rumors have persisted that she was killed by the Ku Klux Klan. Her son Anthony Boone was a senior in high school. One night, she was walking to the football field to see her son playing football. She never made it to the field, as she was run over by a truck. No one was ever charged with a crime. She paid the ultimate sacrifice. She was the daughter of Joseph "Joe" Tillett and Arviller Golden Tillett and the wife of the late Charles Edward Boone. In the 1960s, he was the principal at the Davis School in Engelhard, NC.

African American communities always faced some kind of threat. At the time of the Hyde County boycott, Dare County and other African American communities in North Carolina were threatened to be burned down. Dare County's all-white Commissioners Board wouldn't meet with the African American community. The community demanded that the board let the community know if their lives were in danger. White people feared what would happen in an open public meeting, so the African American community was banned from holding it. The board appointed one person from the community to attend. Virginia Tillett, another trailblazer in the fight for civil rights, sat in the dark as the meeting took place. The meeting ran late into the night, long after nine o'clock. As the hour grew late, Virginia's parents, William Seward and Earlene Bryant Simmons sat at home and prayed for her safety. Earlene talked with Dell throughout the night. She knew Dell's house would be the first place Virginia would stop. She told Dell the Klan had made it to the old bridge at Manns Harbor, only to be met by a group of white men who turned them around, letting the Klan know that they wouldn't allow the Klan to harm Dare County citizens, be they white or African Americans. She was reassured—and wanted her to reassure her community—that everyone could sleep well and that no harm would come to anyone in Dare County. The Klan had come from as far away as Tennessee and Alabama. African American people always had to sit in the dark at night in fear that someone would harm the community. Every Wednesday, the children would get their homework done early, take their baths, and have dinner before dark. The Ku Klux Klan would meet at the back door of the African American community center, at what is now Ace Hardware. One of the white men would ride through the African American community until the meetings were over. We could see the bonfire burning as they held their meetings. The community stayed quiet, and no harm ever came to the people.

Life for African Americans was like a storm surge, the worst part of the hurricane. With no voting rights and low-paying jobs, families wanted a say in their future. All the horror-visited blacks didn't stop the African American community. Everyone continued to fight for their rights, making dreams of a better life more possible. African Americans in Dare County survived the hardships of discrimination and injustice.

In 1967, Dellerva "Dell" Wise Collins became the community service coordinator of the Community Action Agency. She coordinated programs in Dare County, such as Head Start, Section 8 housing, weatherization, childcare, jobs, and housing referral programs. She was assigned to work with low-income families in Dare County, assessing client needs. In a paper, she wrote about her first assignment, doing outreach work in the Manns Harbor, Stumpy Point, and East Lake communities. She was scheduled to meet with a group of clients at a community building about 2 miles off the main highway, in the woods. When reaching the end of the road, she saw a large open field and a building with the letters KKK painted on it. She had heard men talk about doing a donut with their car, not knowing what they meant. She experienced doing a donut herself that day as she sped out of there. This was the first time she felt her life was in danger. Dell had seen a lot growing up, which gave her ample reason to be afraid.

Dell was reassured by her boss that they would never put her in harm's way. The contact client told her that the Klan didn't use the building anymore, that the building was being painted, and to please come back because the people needed her help. When Dell returned, the building had been painted. She and some of the people of the communities became good friends for life.

Dell pushed hard for the Fair Housing Act for residents of Dare County whites and African Americans. Seeing the terrible conditions of some of the people's homes made her drive even harder. Dell bought herself a Porter Roy camera and started taking photographs and writing letters to landlords asking for improvements to the conditions of their properties. If she didn't get results from the landlords, the next step would be to send letters to the Dare County commissioners, Senator Walter B. Jones, and the governor's office. Dell never backed down and always received positive results.

Dell was a people person, showing compassion and love for family and others. She wrote that one of the fondest and most rewarding memories of her job was when a child came and said, "Thank you for the bed. It is the first time I have ever had a bed all to myself."

Another time, she carried clothes to families in Dare County, Hyde County, and Tyrell County. She went outside her county to help the other two poor counties, with few resources for African Americans.

"I have helped people come out of poverty and see the happiness on their faces and the glow in their eyes. It makes my work worthwhile," she wrote.

Dell passed away in 2005. She is missed by her family, friends, and community. There was no problem, big or small, for which Dell couldn't find a positive solution. She was an advocate for low-income families in Dare County, NC. Sometimes, Dell would go into her own pocket to help a person in need. Dell had a heart worth more than gold.

WORKS CITED

Mansa Musa - Wikipedia

   http://en.wikipedia.org/Mansa_Musa

Mansa Musa 1 - World History Encyclopedia

   http://www.worldhistory.org/Mansa_Misa_1

Most Powerful Kings, Queens, Warriors, and Legends

   http://www.ancient-origins.net/history-famous …

7 Most Powerful African Queens

   powerful-African-queens-in-history-you-need-to-know/dwncf5

Ocracoke Newsletter, Slavery on Ocracoke

   http://www.villagecraftsmen.com/news092111.htm

Shell Castle Island

   http://www.coastalreview.org2017/12coasts-history-shell-castle-island

Blount Hall

   http://www.ncpedia.org/blount-hall

ACKNOWLEDGMENTS

To my two beautiful Godchildren, Delroy Bowser, for his help in some of the research, and Elizabeth Bowser, for teaching me how to use the computer to write the book.

To my amazing granddaughters, Kajeria "Kay" Collins and Miniah Collins, for their technology skills in self-editing.

To Josephine Wise Parks, for her true stories of a young girl growing up on the island—the fears, the struggles, and the love of family.

To Jade Haynes, Dare County librarian in Manteo NC, special thanks to you for all your help and kindness.

To my extraordinary, handsome husband, Joseph "Mike" Wilson, for his encouragement and all your love and support.

To my unique, talented, beautiful, and kind daughter, Hananiah Collins, who is always there to help. Thank you for putting together the photographs in this book.

To my awesome son, Cupid Collins, the first to read this book. He said it was good and asked how I collected so much information. "This could be a play, script, maybe even a documentary." His words keep me writing.

To the Memory of Dellerva "Dell" Collins. The bulk of the information in this book came from speeches she gave in church, black history programs, and other research papers she had. She had planned to put together a book herself. When she passed away, I heard her voice saying, "Take what I have given to you to enhance your own life." At the time, I didn't understand what she was saying. Now, it is clear that she wanted me to write this book. I love, miss, and think about my mother every day. She was my best friend, my teacher, and my role model. She was an amazing mother to her two children, Darrell and Yolanda, other family members, and the children's lives she touched in Dare County, black and white. I thank God for the love she had for her family and community and her compassion for humanity. She left behind many batons, and we are all trying to keep her torch lit.

Thanks again to everyone for your support of this book. Your feedback is truly appreciated.

Printed in the United States
by Baker & Taylor Publisher Services